For Nat – J.H.

For Oscar and Beau – G.P.

First published 2021 by Macmillan Children's Books
an imprint of Pan Macmillan
The Smithson, 6 Briset Street, London EC1M 5NR
EU representative: Macmillan Publishers Ireland Ltd, 1st Floor,
The Liffey Trust Centre, 117–126 Sheriff Street Upper,
Dublin 1, DO1 YC43
Associated companies throughout the world.
www.panmacmillan.com

ISBN (PB): 978-1-5290-6316-5
ISBN (Ebook): 978-1-5290-7351-5

3 5 7 9 8 6 4 2

A CIP catalogue record for this book is available from the British Library.

Printed in Spain.

FLY, FLY, FLY YOUR SLEIGH!

John Hay and Garry Parsons

MACMILLAN CHILDREN'S BOOKS

It was nearly Christmas. In Santa's workshop at the North Pole, the elves were rushing around, getting everything ready for the big day.

"Come on, everybody, let's get busy!"
said Holly the Head Elf.

"We've got presents to make.
Then we've got to wrap them and
pack them, and give them to . . ."

"SANTA!"

said all the elves.

"Me?" said Santa.

"No. I don't want them.
Someone else can do
it this year."

"But Santa," said Holly. "You're . . . Santa Claus. You always deliver the presents."

"But I don't want to," said Santa. "I'm fed up with always having to do it."

Holly was worried. Santa wasn't his usual jolly self.
"I know, let's all sing a happy song while we work."

Holly started singing,
and all the elves joined in.

But Santa just sat there
looking grumpy. "I'm not
in the mood for songs,"
he said.

"This is not good,"
said Holly.

Mrs Claus popped her head round the door. "What's going on in here?" she asked.

"It's Santa," said Holly. "He doesn't want to deliver the presents."

"Really?" said Mrs Claus. She plonked a big bowl into Santa's lap. "In that case, he can peel the sprouts!"

"Yum!" said Holly. "All together now . . .

Peel, peel, peel the sprouts,
Cook them till they're done.
If they make you windy,
Please control your bum!

Holly thought she could
hear Santa humming along.
"Feeling better?"

"No," he scowled. "I'm still
not taking the presents."

"Tinsel!" said Holly.
"We have a situation."

Tinsel skipped over to Santa's chair.
"Let's have another song," she said.

♪ Row, row, row your boat, ♩
Gently down the stream.

♪ If you see a polar bear, ♩
Don't forget to scream! ♫

The door flew open, and a huge polar bear ambled into the room. This time, EVERYONE screamed.

"Merry Christmas, Santa," said the polar bear.
"I just popped round to give you your present."

"Thank you," said Santa. "I can't imagine what that is."

Holly looked round the workshop.
It didn't look as festive as usual.

"Hey, elves,"
she said, "why
haven't you hung
your stockings up?"

"Um, because we're still
wearing them?" said Robin.

"That reminds me of a song,"
said Tinsel.

Hang, hang, hang your socks
Yellow, blue or pink.
Don't forget to wash them first,
Or they will really stink!

EEUW!

"Smelly sprouts and stinky socks," sighed Santa. "Delightful!"

Holly was worried.
What else would help
to get Santa into the
right mood?

"Lights!" she said.
"There are no lights
on the tree. Robin,
fetch the ladder."

Robin sang as
he worked.

Light, light, light the lights
All around the tree.
Put the fairy on the top.
Oh no! She needs a wee!

Oops!

"This place is going from
bad to worse," said Santa.
"I'm going to see my
reindeer. At least they
won't sing silly songs."

Outside, some elves were making a snowman.

Roll, roll, roll a ball, Make it out of snow.
Put a hat upon his head . . .

Where does this carrot go?

"Oi," said the snowman.
"Careful with that carrot."

"Santa!" said Ryan the Reindeer. "When do we set off?"

"I thought we'd stay at home this Christmas,"
said Santa. "Have a quiet one."

"No!" said Ryan.
"I love flying round
the world, dropping
off presents, the sleigh
bells jingling . . ."

"Well, you can do it then," said Santa.
"I know what would cheer you up," said Ryan.

"Let's sing a song!"

Row, row, row your boat,
Gently down the stream.
If a penguin says hello,
Give him an ice cream!

"Seriously?"
said Santa, as the
reindeer burst
into song.

"Hello," said a penguin. "I think I'm lost.

But did somebody say ice cream?"

"Good idea," said Holly. "Ice creams all round.
And Tinsel, how about fetching Santa
some milk and cookies?"

"Milk and cookies?"
said Santa.

"Why would I
want milk and
cookies now? I'll
be having them
all around the
world tonight."

"Wait," said Holly. "So you're delivering the presents after all?"

"If it means I don't have to listen to any more songs," said Santa.

"Excellent!" said Holly.
"All together now!"

♫ ♪ Pack, pack, pack your bags, load them on the sleigh— ♪

"What did I say?" roared Santa. And the elves loaded up the presents without another word.

Santa climbed aboard, then the reindeer galloped across the snow, faster and faster until they soared into the sky. As Santa sped away, everyone sang one last song,

Fly, fly, fly your sleigh,
Loaded up with fun.
Merry, Merry, Merry
Merry Christmas everyone!

"I give up," chuckled Santa.